Bunny Lune

by Kae Nishimura

Clarion Books

New York

Clarion Books
a Houghton Mifflin Company imprint
215 Park Avenue South, New York, NY 10003
Copyright © 2007 by Kae Nishimura

The illustrations were executed in watercolor.
The text was set in 16-point Cantoria.

For information about permission to reproduce selections from this book,
write to Permissions, Houghton Mifflin Company, 215 Park Avenue South,
New York, NY 10003.

www.clarionbooks.com

Printed in China

Library of Congress Cataloguing-in-Publication Data

Nishimura, Kae.
Bunny Lune / by Kae Nishimura.
p.   cm.
Summary: When Bunny Lune receives a letter from his friend telling him about the
Japanese moon festival, Bunny cannot stop dreaming about visiting the moon himself.
ISBN-13: 978-0-618-71606-7
ISBN-10: 0-618-71606-8
[1. Moon—Fiction. 2. Rabbits—Fiction.] I. Title.
PZ7.N639Bu 2007
[E]—dc22
2006013666

WKT   10 9 8 7 6 5 4 3 2 1

To the friends who still visit their own moon

One day in September, I got a letter from
my friend Pyonko, who lives in Japan.

Dear Bunny Lune,

Last night my family and I celebrated the full moon with rice dumplings and tea. In Japan, there is a tradition that rabbits live on the moon and make rice dumplings, so it is a special day for us. We sang moon songs. I wish you could have been there. Love xxx

Pyonko

5

The moon! Once I started
thinking about it, I couldn't stop.

The next day, I went to the travel agency
to sign up for a moon tour.

8

"That will be one billion dollars," the travel agent said, looking me over from head to toe.

"I'll think about it and get back to you," I said.

9

One billion dollars!
Everything costs so
much in America.

I wish I lived in Japan.
Then I could visit the
moon for free.

I started my own business selling hard-boiled
eggs to office workers at lunchtime.

"It's too early for rabbits
and Easter eggs,"
they told me.
"Come back in the spring."

13

How was I ever going to earn a billion dollars? I found
a job at a salad bar. I knew I looked silly, but it was a job.

By the end of the day, I was exhausted and I had earned only fifty dollars. That meant I'd have to work 20 million more days—54,794 years—to pay for my moon tour.
I quit the job.

I decided to learn more about the moon. Maybe I could find another way to get there.

I went to the library. *Science Now* said that space travelers had to be trained in gravity-free flight.

I tried the space walk at the amusement park, but it upset my stomach.

Science Today said that there was no air on the moon.

I tried to hold my breath, but I only lasted about a minute.

It was hopeless.
I decided to forget
my dream and
ignore the moon.

18

But everywhere I went,
there were reminders.

I even discovered that the new
pajamas I'd bought had moons on them.

At bedtime, I looked up at the night sky. Thousands of
stars twinkled above, and I saw the constellation Lepus.
What a lucky rabbit—so close to the moon!

20

Finally, I fell asleep, bathed in the light
of the beautiful moon.

The next day, I saw an interesting
poster. "The Mayor of the Moon will
speak," it said. "Come to the park at noon
to hear about his adventures."

I went to the park
and found a crowd
gathered around a
shabby old man.

"I visited the moon for
the first time when I was
twenty years old," the old man
was saying. "That's where I met Diana."
"Excuse me," a young woman interrupted.
"You met someone on the moon?
Are you talking about an alien?"

"No, Diana is my muse, my inspiration," replied the old man. "We fell in love and danced a moon dance together. I wore a tuxedo, of course."

People shook their heads in disbelief.

"You didn't wear a space suit?"
"You danced on the moon?"

"Mayor of the Moon, indeed. You're just a liar."

One by one,
they turned their
backs and walked away.
Finally, I was the only one left.

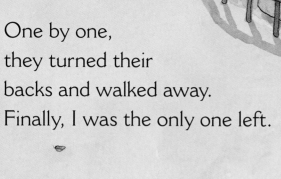